PERCY IN DISGUISE

by
The Rev. W. Awdry

with illustrations by
Gunvor & Peter Edwards

GROLIER

Ghost Train

". . . AND every year on the date of the accident it runs again, plunging into the gap, shrieking like a lost soul."

"Percy, what *are* you talking about?"

"The Ghost Train. Driver saw it last night."

"Where?" asked Thomas and Toby together.

"He didn't say, but it must have been on our line. He says ghost trains run as a warning to others.

"Oooh!" he went on, "it makes my wheels wobble to think of it!"

"Pooh!" said Thomas. "You're just a silly little engine, Percy. I'm not scared."

"Thomas didn't believe in your ghost," said Percy, next morning.

His Driver laughed. "Neither do I. It was a 'pretend' ghost on television."

Percy was disappointed, but he was too busy all day with his stone trucks to think about ghosts. That evening he came back "light engine" from the harbour. He liked running at night. He coasted along without effort, the rails humming cheerfully under his wheels, and signal lights changing to green at his approach.

He always knew just where he was, even in the dark. "Crowe's Farm Crossing," he chuntered happily. "We shan't be long now."

Sam had forgotten that Mr Crowe wanted a load of lime taken to Forty-acre field. When he remembered, it was nearly dark. He drove in a hurry, bumped over the crossing, and sank his cart's front wheels in mud at the field gate.

The horse tried hard, but couldn't move it. The cart's tail still fouled the railway.

Sam gave it up. He unharnessed the horse, and rode back to the farm for help. "There's still time," he told himself. "The next train isn't due for an hour."

But he'd reckoned without Percy.

Percy broke the cart to smithereens, and lime flew everywhere. They found no one at the crossing, so went on to the nearest signalbox.

"Hullo!" said the Signal man. "What have you done to Percy? He's white all over!"

Percy's Driver explained. "I'll see to it," said the Signalman, "but you'd better clean Percy, or people will think he's a ghost!"

Percy chuckled. "Do let's pretend I'm a ghost, and scare Thomas. That'll teach him to say I'm a silly little engine!"

On their way they met Toby, who promised to help.

Thomas was being "oiled up" for his evening

train, when Toby hurried in saying, "Percy's had an accident."

"Poor engine!" said Thomas. "Botheration! That means I'll be late."

"They've cleared the line for you," Toby went on, "but there's something worse –"

"Out with it, Toby," Thomas interrupted. "I can't wait all evening."

" – I've just seen something," said Toby in a shaky voice. "It *looked* like Percy's ghost. It s-said it w-was c-coming here t-to w-warn us."

"Pooh! Who cares? Don't be frightened, Toby. I'll take care of you."

Percy approached the Shed quietly and

glided through it. "Peeeeep! peeeeeeeeeeeep! pip! pip! pip! Peeeeeeeeeeeeeeep!" he shrieked.

As had been arranged, Toby's Driver and Fireman quickly shut the doors.

"Let me in! Let me in!" said Percy in a spooky voice.

"No, no!" answered Toby. "Not by the smoke of my chimney, chim chim!"

"I'll chuff and I'll puff, and I'll break your door in!"

"Oh dear!" exclaimed Thomas. "It's getting late . . . I'd no idea . . . I must find Annie and Clarabel . . ."

He hurried out the other way.

Percy was none the worse for his adventure. He was soon cleaned; but Thomas never returned. Next morning Toby asked him where he'd been.

"Ah well," said Thomas. "I knew you'd be sad about Percy, and – er – I didn't like to – er – intrude. I slept in the Goods Shed, and . . . Oh!" he went on hurriedly, "sorry . . . can't stop . . . got to see a coach about a train," and he shot off like a jack rabbit.

Percy rolled up alongside. "Well! Well! Well!" he exclaimed. "What d'you know about that?"

"Anyone would think," chuckled Toby, "that our Thomas had just seen a ghost!"

Woolly Bear

GANGERS had been cutting the line-side grass and "cocking" it.

The Fat Controller sells the hay to hill-farmers who want winter feed for their stock.

At this time of year, when Percy comes back from the harbour, he stops where they have been cutting. The men load up his empty wagons, and he pulls them to Ffarquhar. Toby then takes them to the hills. The farmers collect the hay from Toby's top station.

When in the wagons, the hay is covered to prevent it blowing about, but on the line-side it is stacked in the open air to dry.

"Wheeeeeeeeeeesh!" Percy gave his ghostly whistle. "Don't be frightened, Thomas," he laughed, "it's only me!"

"Your ugly fizz is enough to frighten anyone," said Thomas crossly. "You're like – "

"Ugly indeed! I'm – "

" – a green caterpillar with red stripes," continued Thomas firmly. "You crawl like one too."

"I don't."

"Who's been late every afternoon this week?"

"It's the hay."

"I can't help that," said Thomas. "Time's time, and the Fat Controller relies on me to keep it. I can't if you crawl in the hay till all hours."

"Green caterpillar indeed!" fumed Percy. "Everyone says I'm handsome – or at least *nearly* everyone. Anyway, my curves are better than Thomas' corners."

He took his trucks to the harbour, and spent the morning shunting. "Thomas says I'm always late," he grumbled. "I'm never late – or at least only a few minutes. What's that to Thomas? He can always catch up time further on."

All the same, he and his Driver decided to start home early. It was most unfortunate that, just before they did, a crate of treacle was upset over him. They wiped the worst off, but he was still sticky when he puffed away.

The wind rose as they puffed along. Soon it was blowing a gale.

"Look at that!" exclaimed his Driver.

The wind caught the piled hay, tossing it up and over the track. The gangers tried to clear it, but more always came.

The line climbed here. "Take a run at it Percy," his Driver advised; so, whistling warningly, Percy gathered speed. But the hay made the rails slippery, and his wheels wouldn't grip. Time after time he stalled with spinning wheels and had to wait till the line ahead was cleared before he could start again.

The Signalman climbed a telegraph pole, the Stationmaster paced the platform, passengers fussed, and Thomas seethed impatiently.

"Ten minutes late! I warned him. Passengers'll complain, and the Fat Controller . . ."

The Signalman shouted, the Stationmaster stood amazed, the passengers exclaimed and laughed as Percy approached.

"Sorry – I'm – late!" Percy panted.

"So I should hope," scolded Thomas; but he spoilt the effect as Percy drew alongside. "Look what's crawled out of the hay!" he chortled.

"What's wrong?" asked Percy.

"Talk about hairy caterpillars!" puffed

Thomas as he started away. "It's worth being late to have seen you!"

When Percy got home his Driver showed him what he looked like in a mirror.

"Bust my buffers!" exclaimed Percy. "No wonder they all laughed. I'm just like a woolly bear! Please clean me before Toby comes."

But it was no good. Thomas told Toby all about it, and instead of talking about sensible things like playing ghosts, Thomas and Toby made jokes about "woolly bear" caterpillars and other creatures which crawl about in hay.

They laughed a lot, but Percy thought they were really being very silly indeed.